VAN BUREN
DECATUR
W9-ASD-522

Frankenstein
Doesn't Start
Food Fights

DISCARDED

Want more Bailey School Kids?
Check these out!

 #1-47

SUPER SPECIALS #1-6

 #1-10

And don't miss the...

HOLIDAY SPECIALS

Swamp Monsters Don't Chase Wild Turkeys
Aliens Don't Carve Jack-o'-lanterns
Mrs. Claus Doesn't Climb Telephone Poles
Leprechauns Don't Play Fetch
Ogres Don't Hunt Easter Eggs

VAN BUREN DISTRICT LIBRARY
MICHIGAN

Frankenstein Doesn't Start Food Fights

by Debbie Dadey
and
Marcia Thornton Jones

illustrated by John Steven Gurney

A
LITTLE APPLE
PAPERBACK

SCHOLASTIC INC.
New York   Toronto   London   Auckland   Sydney
Mexico City   New Delhi   Hong Kong   Buenos Aires

Dad

*To my Colorado critique group: Lynn Dean, Sally
Kelly Engeman, Jean Bell, Helen Colella, Linda
Osmundson, LeAnn Thieman, Kerrie Flanagan, Ellen
Javernick, Carol Steward, and Carol Rehme.*
— DD

*To Barbara Underhill: a true friend who knows
how to cook up a monstrously good time!*
— MTJ

If you purchased this book without a cover, you should be aware that this
book is stolen property. It was reported as "unsold and destroyed" to the
publisher, and neither the author nor the publisher has received any
payment for this "stripped book."

No part of this publication may be reproduced in whole or in part, stored
in a retrieval system, or transmitted in any form or by any means,
electronic, mechanical, photocopying, recording, or otherwise, without
written permission of the publisher. For information regarding permission,
write to Scholastic Inc., Attention: Permissions Department, 557 Broadway,
New York, NY 10012.

ISBN 0-439-55999-5

Text copyright © 2003 by Marcia Thornton Jones and Debra S. Dadey.
Illustrations copyright © 2003 by Scholastic Inc.

All rights reserved. Published by Scholastic Inc.

SCHOLASTIC, LITTLE APPLE, THE ADVENTURES OF THE BAILEY SCHOOL KIDS,
and associated logos are trademarks and/or registered trademarks of
Scholastic Inc.

12 11 10 9 8 7 6 5 4   3 4 5 6 7 8/0

Printed in the U.S.A.   40

First printing, September 2003

Contents

1

Football

"Think fast!" Eddie threw the ball to Howie. Eddie and his best friends, Howie, Liza, and Melody, were on the playground near a big oak tree before school started. Red and orange leaves crunched beneath their feet.

Howie tried to catch the ball, but Melody was too fast. She snatched it out of the air and tossed it to Liza.

"Throw me that ball!" Eddie yelled.

Liza passed it to him, all right. She tossed it right at his face. "Oops, sorry," Liza said as the ball bounced off Eddie's nose.

"It didn't hurt," Eddie said, even though his nose had turned bright red. "But that's exactly why girls shouldn't play football."

Melody put her hands on her hips and

glared at Eddie. "Girls can do anything that boys can do, only better."

"Nuh-uh," Eddie argued as he danced around Melody. "Boys are better than girls are. Boys are better than girls are!"

"Eddie," Melody said. "You are such a pain."

"That's me," Eddie said. "Eddie, the pain." He grabbed the football and threw it to Howie.

Smack! The ball hit Howie in the stomach and knocked him to the ground.

"Are you all right?" Liza asked.

Howie gasped for breath and nodded.

Melody frowned and helped Howie up. "You shouldn't be so rough," she said to Eddie. "Are you trying to hurt Howie?"

Eddie shook his head. "No, I'm trying to help him. He has to get in shape so we can try out for the junior high football team together."

"We're only in elementary school," Liza said. "I don't think third graders can play for the Bailey City Junior High team."

"No kidding," Eddie said. "We have to practice now if we want to be great by sixth grade."

Eddie snatched the ball off the ground and tossed it high in the air. "Howie," Eddie yelled. "Go long."

Howie ran a long way, but not long enough. Somebody caught the football, and it wasn't Howie.

The person holding the football towered over Howie, blocking out the sun. Liza almost fainted. Eddie and Melody gulped.

Howie screamed.

2

Frank

"AHHHH!" Howie screamed.

He tried to stop. His sneakers slid through the dirt on the playground, sending up a dust cloud. But he was too late. Howie crashed into a towering giant of a man. It was like running into a brick wall, and Howie ended up flat on the ground.

When the giant man held up the football, Liza couldn't help noticing the jagged scar on his wrist. The man's long legs stuck out of brown ragged pants, and a wrinkled white shirt stretched across his broad chest. A huge purple scar covered the left cheek of his pale, square face. A big metal box sat on the ground beside him.

"HRRRRRMM!" the man roared as he

tossed the football across the field. Eddie had to run fast and far to catch it.

"It's Frank!" Liza yelped.

"What's he doing at Bailey Elementary?" Melody wondered. "Why doesn't he stay at the ice-skating rink where he belongs?"

"Why doesn't he stay in the mad scientist's lab where he *really* belongs?" Liza whispered.

Eddie jogged up to the girls, the football tucked under his arm. "He doesn't belong in a lab or a skating rink," Eddie said. "Frank belongs in a dark haunted castle with other monsters."

"Shh," Liza said. "You'll hurt his feelings."

"I thought Frank moved to New York," Eddie said, ignoring Liza. The kids had first met Frank at the Shelley Museum, a nearby nature museum. There they had also met the crazy scientist Dr. Victor. The kids believed Frank was really Frankenstein's monster and that Dr. Victor had pieced Frank together in his secret laboratory. They were sure Dr. Victor and Frank wanted to turn Bailey City into a city full of monsters.

"What about Electra?" Melody asked, remembering the lady who had baked cookies at the skating rink. Frank had started teaching hockey at the skating rink after a huge fight with Dr. Victor. Frank met Electra while working at the rink and fell in love with her. "Didn't they get married?"

Liza shrugged. "Maybe it didn't work out between the two of them."

"What's not to work out?" Eddie said. "They're both monsters; they were perfect for each other."

"Eddie, that's not very nice," Liza told her friend. "People can't help what they look like. Some people might think you look like a monster."

Melody giggled. "Most people think Eddie *acts* like a monster."

Eddie held up his fist at Melody, but

Liza stepped in between the two of them. "Come on, you guys," Liza said. "This is no time to argue. Let's go see what Frank is up to."

"Maybe Frank just likes to play football," Eddie said.

"Must be a monster thing," Melody teased.

Liza folded her arms across her chest. "Why are you two always picking on each other? My mom said that sometimes people tease the ones they have a crush on. I bet that's the reason for all your teasing. You're flirting with each other!"

Eddie spit on the ground. "Yuck! Flirting is disgusting."

"I totally agree," Melody said, grabbing the football out of Eddie's arms. "I'd rather eat a bucket of slimy worms than flirt with Eddie."

Eddie, Melody, and Liza were so busy arguing, they had forgotten all about Howie until they heard a loud thud.

"Uh-oh, sounds like Howie's in trouble," Liza told her friends. "We'd better go rescue him."

Melody looked across the playground. "I think we're already too late," she gasped.

3

Monster Mash

"Where did they go?" Eddie asked.

The kids stared across the playground. "They're gone," Melody said.

"Frank stole Howie!" Liza gasped. "He's taken him back to the mad scientist's laboratory. What if Frank turns Howie into a mini-monster?"

"Don't jump to conclusions," Melody said.

"Melody's right," Eddie said. "They can't have gone too far. We can still catch up to them. Howie has nothing to worry about with me around. I'll find that kid-stealing monster and tackle him to the ground."

Eddie snatched his football from Melody and raced across the playground. She and Liza ran after him. The ground was scuffed where Howie had fallen, but other than that, there was no sign of their friend — and no sign of a monster, either.

"Where did they go?" Liza asked after she caught her breath.

Eddie held his finger to his lips to keep his friends quiet. Then he slowly turned in a circle, looking in every direction. "There is only one place they could be," Eddie finally said. He pointed to the double doors that led into Bailey Elementary School.

"We're not allowed to go inside before the bell rings," Liza reminded him.

"Rules don't count when a friend is in trouble," Melody said.

Eddie shoved his ball cap down over his curly red hair and nodded. "She's right. Rules don't count. Now let's do it!"

The door closed behind them with a definite thud. Inside, the hallway was totally deserted.

"I don't like this," Liza whispered.

"It's even worse knowing Howie is

trapped inside with a monster," Melody told her.

"The idea of being trapped inside a school with teachers is bad enough to give me nightmares for a month," Eddie said. "Monsters just make it worse."

A door down the hallway suddenly slammed shut and something crashed to the floor. "I think they went that way," Melody said.

"Then that's the way we go," Eddie said in his bravest voice.

Eddie, Melody, and Liza crept down the gloomy hallway. Shadows loomed all around them and a strange creaking noise filled the air.

"That must be the sound of Frank's monster-making machine," Liza said. "Poor Howie!"

"Don't be silly," Melody answered. "I'm sure Howie is perfectly fine." But she hurried toward the noise.

"It's coming from the cafeteria," Eddie said.

"This is worse than I imagined," Liza whimpered. "Frank isn't turning Howie into a monster. He's turning Howie into monster mash!"

Melody grabbed the cafeteria door and pulled hard. "Not if I can help it!"

4

Poison

"HHHRRRRMMM!" Frank roared as the three kids threw open the door. The giant man covered his eyes when Eddie flipped on the light switch. Frank stumbled back into the shadows of the kitchen.

"Howie!" Liza screamed. "We're here to save you!"

Howie looked up from a huge cookie he was holding. "Save me?" he asked. "From what? Sugar and spices? Chocolate chips and butterscotch morsels?"

"We thought you were being turned into monster mash," Melody whispered. "We didn't know you were getting a monster treat."

"We were worried sick about you," Liza said. "Why did you disappear like that?"

"Sorry," he said. "Frank asked me to show him to the cafeteria."

Frank peered around the kitchen door at the four kids. "Hhhrrrmm?" Frank's groan ended in a question.

"It's okay," Howie told Frank. "They were just wondering where I went."

The big man cautiously stepped out from the kitchen. His shoe hit the floor so hard it echoed throughout the empty cafeteria.

Liza poked Howie in the side. "Don't you know better than to go off with strangers?" she asked under her breath.

Howie grinned. "This is no stranger. This is Frank. You remember when he taught us how to play ice hockey, don't you?"

"We remember only too well," Melody said. "We also remember when he and Dr. Victor worked together at the museum and they made that Formula Big."

"Hello," Liza said politely as Frank took another step closer.

Eddie wasn't so polite. "What are you doing at our school? We thought you were moving to New York."

Frank slowly smiled, showing a huge row of yellow teeth. "Research," he grunted. "Must do research. My new wife, Electra, likes children. Little children. Big children. All children. She plans to sell cookies. In schools. Your school will be the test."

"Awesome!" Eddie said. "I love Electra's cookies even more than I like football." The sight of the cookies made Eddie forget all about monsters.

All the kids had tasted Electra's cookies when she opened a bakery at the skating rink. They were delicious and very big.

"Electra worked hard. Made her cookies healthier," Frank explained as Eddie helped himself to a cookie from the large platter. "Healthy makes kids big and strong. She experimented in her very own laboratory."

"Football players need to be big and strong," Eddie bragged. "Just like me."

Eddie didn't want to hear about research. He didn't want to know about Electra's laboratory. He didn't care about healthy, but he did like cookies. He stuffed a cookie into his mouth and chewed. His eyes grew big. His face grew so pale his freckles stood out. Then he spit out every bit of cookie.

"It's poison!" he moaned, grabbing his neck and falling to the floor. "Poison!"

5

Cookies

"I admit they aren't as good as Electra's chocolate chip, but her new cookies aren't that bad," Howie said later as the kids walked into their classroom. All around them other kids sat down in their seats.

"You never even tasted your cookie," Eddie said.

Howie shrugged. "I did take a little bite, but I didn't want any more after you said they tasted like poison."

"I think it's nice that Frank and Electra are trying to make their cookies healthier," Liza said.

Eddie made a face and stuck out his tongue. "Cookies are not meant to be healthy," he snapped. "They are supposed to taste good, good, good."

Melody shook her head. "Things can taste good and be healthy for you, too."

"Like bananas," Howie said.

"Yeah, if you're a monkey," Eddie said. He put his hands in his armpits and made monkey grunts.

"Eddie, stop monkeying around," Liza said with a giggle.

"Apples are healthy and you like them," Melody reminded Eddie.

Eddie rolled his eyes and fell into his seat. "Healthy, smealthy," he groaned. "I just want good."

"*Shhh*," Liza warned. "Here comes Mrs. Jeepers."

"I'm not afraid of her," Eddie bragged. "I'm not afraid of anyone." He said it, but he said it very quietly.

When their teacher, Mrs. Jeepers, walked into the room, all the kids grew quiet. There was something about their teacher that made everyone behave. Maybe it was the mysterious brooch she wore, or maybe it was the fact that some

kids thought she was a vampire. After all, she did live in a haunted house. She had even moved to Bailey City from Transylvania, where Count Dracula had lived.

"Children," Mrs. Jeepers said, her green eyes flashing. "I have a surprise for you."

Liza smiled. She loved surprises, but Eddie groaned. He had a feeling that Mrs. Jeepers' surprise was not going to be the kind that he liked.

He was right.

6

Cookie Monsters

The next morning on the way to school, Eddie complained to his friends. "A surprise is a new bike or a trip to Disney World or the Super Bowl."

Melody nodded in agreement. "A surprise should be something fun, like a soccer tournament or a field trip to a horse farm."

"Testing Frank's poison cookies will NOT be fun!" Eddie yelled to the whole neighborhood.

A few dogs barked back at Eddie, but Liza giggled. "Oh, come on, the cookies can't be that bad," she said. "Besides, the whole school has to do it."

Eddie pretended to gag. "If you had onions and mixed them with mud, it would taste better than Frank's new cookies," he said. "But turning cookie tasting into a math project is the worst idea I've ever heard. Only a teacher could think that was a surprise."

"Studying charts can be pretty interesting," Howie said. "Even football coaches keep charts. Our chart will keep track of which cookies taste the best."

"We could become famous as the school who rated the best-selling brand of Monster Cookies," Liza said.

Melody nodded. "The TV station might even interview us."

"Maybe that pretty reporter from WMTJ will ask us questions," Liza said as she stopped to look both ways before crossing Delaware Boulevard.

"Big fat chance of that," Eddie said. "Frank is just using our school to test his cookies for free."

"Speaking of Frank," Melody said, turning toward Howie. "What was that horrible noise coming from the cafeteria yesterday when you were with Frank?"

"Whatever it was," Howie said, "it was coming from the big blue metal box in the kitchen."

"What was inside it?" Liza asked.

Howie shrugged. "Frank carried it into the kitchen so I couldn't see."

"That's probably where he keeps the poison," Eddie said.

"I tasted a cookie," Howie said, "and it didn't make me sick."

"You must have to eat a bunch of them," Eddie said. "It must be a cumulonimbus effect."

"You mean cumulative," Howie corrected Eddie.

"We'll have to taste so many cookies, we'll turn into cookie monsters. Oh, no," Eddie said. "That's it!"

"What?" Liza said.

"Frank is trying to poison all the kids at Bailey School!" Eddie told his friends.

"You're crazy," Melody told Eddie. The kids dropped their backpacks under the

big oak tree on the playground. "Principal Davis would never allow a monster to bring poison into our school."

"I'm not talking about your everyday bad-tasting poison. I'm talking about mad-scientist stuff," Eddie explained. "A formula made just to turn sweet, innocent kids like me into monsters."

"Then it's already working," Liza said with a giggle, "because the sweet, innocent Eddie was replaced by a horrible monster years ago. Just ask any teacher and they'll tell you it's true."

"Very funny, monster breath," Eddie said. "But you won't be laughing when Frank and his monster wife turn every Bailey School kid into big hairy monsters with warts, using Dr. Victor's newest secret formula."

Howie slumped against the side of the tree like he was thinking hard. "Eddie may be onto something," Howie whispered. "Frank *is* a friend of Dr. Victor."

"That's right, and we all know that Dr.

Victor is some kind of mad scientist," Eddie said. "Dr. Victor, Frank, and Electra have cooked up a cookie-flavored monster formula." Eddie pounded his fist into his other hand. "It's up to us to do something about it!"

7

Electra

All morning, Eddie had thought about his monster-formula idea. Thanks to Eddie, the rest of his friends had thought about it, too. That's because Eddie wouldn't stop talking about it. At lunchtime, Liza, Melody, Howie, and Eddie sat at a corner table by themselves.

Liza pointed a carrot at Eddie's nose. "Why would Frank put a monster formula in the cookies?" she asked.

"Why do birds fly? Why do dogs shed? Why does Dracula suck blood?" Eddie asked Liza, but he didn't give her time to answer. "You want to know why? I'll tell you why. It's just what monsters and mad scientists do."

"And why does Eddie keep talking when he isn't making any sense? Because he's as nutty as the peanut butter in my

31

sandwich, that's why!" Howie blurted, holding up his half-eaten sandwich.

All around them kids hurried to eat sandwiches and sip milk as if nothing out of the ordinary was happening at their school. Then they rushed to get in line at the back of the cafeteria where Frank and Electra stood behind a long table. The mysterious blue metal box sat at the end of the table. It rattled and shook and belched.

The kids had met Electra before, but they still couldn't get over the way she looked. Electra stood nearly as tall as Frank. Her hair was piled so high on her head she could've hidden three cats and a hamster in it.

Frank stood behind Electra, watching his wife as she worked. Mountains of giant cookies filled the tray in front of them. Electra carefully handed out cookies to a line of third graders and waited for them to be tasted. Kid after kid took bites and told her what they thought of

the new cookies. Each time, Frank made a mark on a giant chart taped to the wall.

"We have to remember to study Frank's chart before we go back to math class," Howie noted.

"Those poor kids," Eddie said with a shake of his head. "With every bite, they're soaking up more and more of Dr. Victor's monster-making formula."

"Frank said Electra was trying to make the cookies healthy," Liza pointed out. "Maybe the formula is nothing more than whole wheat and oatmeal."

"Don't you remember Formula Big?" Eddie sputtered. "And what about Super Hockey Formula B?"

The kids all thought back to the time when they believed Dr. Victor was using a special formula to grow giant flowers. They also thought Frank had stolen Dr. Victor's special formula and used it to turn ordinary hockey players into superstars on ice.

"This cookie formula could be even

worse," Eddie continued. "And I bet Frank's mixing up the formula in that high-tech metal box."

"Frank did say healthy food made kids big and strong," Liza said. "Maybe he's using Dr. Victor's Formula Big to turn us into monsters."

"There are other things that are big and strong besides monsters," Melody pointed out. "Like trees."

"Great," Eddie said. "If Electra and Frank are mixing Formula B for Bark into those cookies, we'll all be growing branches out our ears and sprouting leaves out our noses."

"You don't really think we're all going to be turned into maple trees," Liza asked, "do you?"

"Of course not," Howie said. "But if Eddie's right, then kids will soon start to show signs of the formula working. All we have to do is watch to see if the kids who eat cookies start acting strange."

"Or looking strange!" added Liza.

The kids glanced around the cafeteria. Ben, a fourth grader, was pinching a girl named Issy. "Maybe Frank is using Formula Shellfish and turning us all into pinching crabs," Liza whispered.

Melody shook her head. "Ben always acts like that."

"What about Carey?" Howie asked.

The other three kids looked at a girl with curly hair and glasses. She stared back at them, batting her eyelashes at Eddie.

"When she blinks like that, she looks like a giant toad," Eddie said with a laugh.

Liza's face grew as pale as the napkin on her tray. "Maybe Frank's formula is turning us into wart-covered frogs."

Howie patted Liza on the shoulder. "Stop worrying. Carey always bats her eyes."

"I know what it is!" Melody exclaimed.

She slapped her hand on the table and knocked her milk carton over.

"What?" Eddie, Liza, and Howie asked Melody.

"It's Formula C for crazy, because that's what all of you are. Crazy," Melody said, getting up from the lunch table. "Electra and Frank are conducting a scientific test to see which cookies will be popular with kids. That's all there is to it, and I'm going to eat one of those cookies right now before they're all gone!"

"No!" Eddie called, but he was too late.

Melody had already hopped up from the table and skipped across the cafeteria. She was next in line to get a monster-sized cookie.

"We have to stop her," Eddie told Howie and Liza. "Those cookies are bound to be full of Dr. Victor's horrible secret ingredient. There's no telling what it will do to Melody."

Eddie didn't wait for his friends to join him. He ran across the room and grabbed the cookie right out of Melody's mouth.

"AAAAHHHHH!" Electra screamed. Her voice was so high and loud Liza had to cover her ears. "My cookies! My cookies! What are you doing to my cookies?"

At the sound of Electra's scream, Frank roared. "HHHHRRRRMMM!" He pushed the table aside, sending the tray of cookies crashing to the floor. Two giant steps later he towered over Eddie.

"Stealing bad," Frank howled. "Stealing very bad!" Slowly, he reached down

and lifted Eddie up by the back of his shirt.

"I . . . I . . . I'm sorry," Eddie stammered. "I won't steal any cookies ever again."

Frank didn't put Eddie down. Instead, Frank held Eddie as if he were holding a mouse by the tail and carried him out the cafeteria door.

8

Crumb History

"Oh, no," Melody said. "Eddie's really done it now."

"What do you think Frank will do to him?" Liza asked. She sniffed and touched a napkin to her nose. Her nose tended to bleed when she got upset.

"Whatever it is, it can't be good," Howie said.

"Come on," Melody told her friends. "It's up to us to save Eddie."

The three kids ran to the cafeteria door just as Eddie rushed back in. He pushed Melody and Howie aside. "Out of my way," Eddie yelled. "I've got a school to save."

Eddie was halfway across the floor when Frank slammed through the doors. "HHHRRRRMMM!" Frank roared and pointed at Eddie. "Stop him!"

Electra's eyes flashed. She reached her arms out toward Eddie.

"You're surrounded, Eddie," Liza yelled. "Run!"

Eddie didn't run. Instead, he screeched to a stop right in the middle of the floor.

Frank and Electra moved closer and closer.

"What is Eddie doing?" Melody yelped.

"They're going to turn him into a monster sandwich," Howie moaned. "And there's nothing we can do to save him."

Step by step, Frank and Electra closed in on Eddie.

Just as their fingers were about to close around his collar, Eddie went into football mode. He ducked low and dodged to the right as if he were avoiding a tackle. Then he fell to the floor and rolled safely away. He moved so fast, Frank and Electra didn't have time to stop. They crashed into each other so hard they both fell to the floor in a heap — a giant heap.

Eddie scrambled up from the floor and raced across the cafeteria. He quickly used one of the trays to scoop up the cookies from the floor.

"Hurry, Eddie," Liza screamed.

"Watch out behind you," Howie warned.

Eddie faced Frank and Electra. They had pulled themselves up from the floor and were making their way toward Eddie.

"Come one step closer," Eddie said, "and these cookies are history. Crumb history."

Electra threw back her head and shrieked, "My cookies! Give me my cookies!"

Frank reached for the tray. "COOK-IES!" He tried to yank the tray away from Eddie, but Eddie held on tight. The tray stayed in Eddie's hands, but the cookies flew through the air. One cookie landed right on the head of a fourth grader named Ben.

"Fight!" Ben yelled. "Food fight!"

9

Food Fight

"Stop!" Liza screamed as food flew around the cafeteria. All over the room, kids threw their lunches at their friends. Melody ducked right before a blob of mashed potatoes could hit her in the face. They hit Howie instead.

Melody laughed. "You look like an out-of-work Santa Claus."

"Oh, yeah?" Howie said, scraping a handful of mashed potatoes off his face. "Let's see how you'd look as Mrs. Claus."

Howie took off across the cafeteria chasing Melody. They raced past other kids who were screaming and laughing and tossing food.

Eddie was having a great time, throwing food at everyone. "Go long!" Eddie laughed and splashed milk at Ben.

Ben used a straw to blow mashed potatoes at Eddie.

"Wow, that's a great idea," Eddie said. Eddie looked for a straw on the table near him, but when he couldn't find one he blasted Frank in the nose with a spoonful of green beans instead. Then he hit a girl named Carey in the back with a hunk of meat loaf.

"Roar!" Frank held a huge pan of mashed potatoes over his head. He grunted and lunged for Eddie.

"Look out!" Liza squealed. "You're about to get creamed."

Howie laughed. "Eddie needs some butter to go with those creamed potatoes."

"This isn't funny," Liza said, wiping a blob of mustard off her chin. "It's dangerous. If Frank hits Eddie with that tray of potatoes, Eddie might really get hurt."

"I don't think so," Melody said. "No kid has ever landed in the hospital from a spud attack."

Liza grabbed Howie's green-bean-crusted arm. "I'm serious," she said. "We have to stop this food fight before someone gets hurt."

Melody looked around the room and saw what she needed. Within two seconds she grabbed a banana and tossed it in front of Frank.

Liza held her breath as Frank held the potato pan high over his head. He was

only seconds away from blasting Eddie into Spudsville. Then came the moment that Melody had hoped for — Frank took one more step and slipped on the banana peel.

Frank slid across the floor. The potatoes and the pan flew up in the air. Frank landed first. The potatoes landed with a splat on Frank's head. And then the pan clanged down right on top of Frank's square-shaped head.

"Ouch," Howie said. "That must have hurt."

"Oh, no," Liza gasped. "I think that just made Frank madder."

10

Potato Skiing

Frank lunged toward Eddie again. Eddie ran from Frank and slipped on a pile of mashed potatoes. "Help!" Eddie screamed.

Eddie slid across the cafeteria. He slid past Ben and Carey, past Melody and Howie. Eddie slid past the whole third grade. Mashed potatoes flew from his feet as if he were water-skiing. "I can't stop," he screamed. "The potatoes are out of control! Holy Toledo!"

"I think Eddie's the one that's out of control," Melody said as Eddie knocked into a cafeteria table. Frank's blue box slid off the table right toward Eddie.

"Look out!" Frank yelled, pulling Eddie out of the way just as the heavy metal box crashed to the floor. Pieces of the

blue box popped off and clattered all around.

"NO!" Frank yelled.

"My cookie oven," Electra sobbed. She fell to the floor and tried to put the pieces back together, but it was useless. The oven had been destroyed.

"Oven?" Eddie squeaked.

Electra sobbed and picked up the chart off the floor. It had been completely destroyed by chocolate milk. It was impossible to see which cookie was the kids' favorite. With a huge sigh Electra tossed the chart into the nearest trash can.

Frank roared and threw back his head. "Arghhh!" he roared.

Eddie shivered and wondered if perhaps, just perhaps, he might have overreacted about the whole secret-formula thing.

At that exact instant, Mrs. Jeepers walked into the cafeteria. After just one look, she rubbed the green brooch she always wore and her eyes flashed.

"Enough," she said quietly.

Every kid in the cafeteria dropped the food that they had been going to throw and gulped. Food covered every square inch of the lunchroom. Peanut butter and jelly sandwiches stuck to the walls and spaghetti hung from the light fixtures. Someone had even managed to get a banana peel up on the picture of the principal. It stuck to the top of his bald head like a rubber wig.

"Oh, my gosh," Liza whispered. "There's Dr. Victor."

The kids were surprised to see the scientist standing beside Mrs. Jeepers. He was a short man with a long nose, funny little glasses, and a white lab coat.

"Dr. Victor's here to see how his formula is working on us," Eddie whispered.

The four friends looked at Mrs. Jeepers and then at Dr. Victor. Neither of the adults smiled. In fact, they looked downright angry. Howie knew that having an

angry vampire and a mad scientist was definitely not a good thing.

Liza stepped behind Melody. "What's Mrs. Jeepers going to do to us?" Liza gasped.

11

Cleanup

It was later in the afternoon and the kids were in the cafeteria scraping dried food off the floor and walls as punishment for the food fight. Other kids grumbled all around them as they wiped off tables and mopped the floor.

Nobody complained as much as Eddie, though. "I repeat," Eddie said. "Surprises are fun. Surprises are not moldy yucky-tasting cookies that you have to scrape off the wall after a food fight."

Liza glared at Eddie. "We should be glad we're still alive. I thought Mrs. Jeepers was going to turn us into toads or something even worse."

"This is all Frank's fault," Eddie snapped. "All I wanted to do was play football. I never wanted to have a food fight. If Frank had stayed in New York, none of this would have happened."

"Frank didn't start the food fight," Howie said.

"That's right," Melody said, tossing a piece of stale bread into the trash and wiping her hands on her jeans. "Frankenstein doesn't start food fights, but Eddie sure does."

"I was only trying to save the school," Eddie said.

"I guess you meant well," Liza admitted. "You were trying to save Melody from getting hurt."

"You saved us, all right," Melody said. "Now we'll probably never get to eat another cookie ever again."

Liza pulled a long strand of spaghetti off her head. "I may never get all this gunk out of my hair," she complained. "I'm definitely going to have to take a bath tonight."

"Yeah," Melody said to Eddie, picking a

green bean out of her black hair, "thanks a lot."

"Eddie should thank Frank," Howie told them.

"Thank Frankenstein?" Eddie said. "For what?"

"He saved your life," Liza said. "If that cookie oven had fallen on you, you might have been crushed."

"Maybe he wasn't trying to poison us after all," Eddie admitted.

"I bet he's really mad at you," Melody said. "After all, you did break his oven and ruin his cookie experiment."

"I think we're about to find out," Liza said. "Frank is coming this way."

12

Monster Idea

Frank pushed through the cafeteria door and came closer and closer to Eddie. Each step of his heavy shoes shook the floor. Glasses rattled on shelves and dishes clanked.

Eddie seemed to shrink as Frank approached.

Melody whimpered. Howie looked like he was praying. Liza covered her face with her hands.

Frank didn't say a word until he was standing right beside Eddie.

Eddie stared up, up, up at Frank's face. "Hi!" Eddie squeaked.

"Grrrr," Frank grunted.

"I . . . I . . . I'm sorry about your cookie oven," Eddie stammered. "I didn't mean to break it. Really, I didn't. I just got carried away with my football moves."

"Carried away," Frank grunted with a nod. Then he shrugged his massive shoulders. "Bailey School kids not ready for healthy cookies. They think healthy bad. Big and strong bad. All very bad."

"Actually," Eddie said, "big and strong isn't that bad. Football players are big and strong. Like me. That's how I broke that oven. I was just too strong."

"You were clumsy," Melody muttered, but Frank didn't hear her.

Frank's eyes grew big. Then he bent down so that his nose nearly touched Eddie's nose. When Frank reached toward Eddie, Eddie closed his eyes tight.

"This is the end," Liza squealed as she peeked through her fingers.

But Liza was wrong. Frank didn't pound Eddie into the ground. He didn't toss Eddie across the room. In fact, Frank didn't act like a monster at all. Instead, he patted Eddie on the head three times. When Frank grinned, the scar on his cheek turned a bright pink. Then Frank turned and stomped out of the cafeteria.

Two months later, Eddie ran onto the playground before school started. "You'll never believe it!" he shouted to his friends. In his hand he held a big box of cookies.

"Wow," Howie said when he saw the picture on the box.

Melody grabbed the package and pulled out a huge football-shaped cookie. She took a bite and smiled. "These are great."

"Of course they are," Eddie said with a smile. "Frank and Electra got the idea from me. They're called Eddie's Really Big Football Cookies. And the best part is, they're not healthy at all!"

"I guess that makes Eddie famous," Liza said.

Melody winked. "That makes Eddie lucky."

Howie sniffed one of the really big cookies. "Do you think these cookies have a secret formula in them?"

"Oh, no!" Liza said, slapping her forehead with her hand. "Here we go again!"

Debbie Dadey and Marcia Thornton Jones have fun writing stories together. When they both worked at an elementary school in Lexington, Kentucky, Debbie was the school librarian and Marcia was a teacher. During their lunch break in the school cafeteria, they came up with the idea of the Bailey School Kids.

Recently Debbie and her family moved to Fort Collins, Colorado. Marcia and her husband still live in Kentucky, where she continues to teach. How do these authors write together? They talk on the phone and use computers and fax machines!

Learn more about Debbie and Marcia at their Web site, www.BaileyKids.com!

Ready for some spooky fun?

Ghostville Elementary™

**from best-selling authors,
Marcia Thornton Jones and Debbie Dadey!**

The basement of Sleepy Hollow's elementary school is haunted. At least that's what everyone says. But no one has ever gone downstairs to prove it. Until now . . .

This year, Cassidy and Jeff's classroom is in the basement. But the kids aren't scared. There's no such thing as ghosts, right?

Tell that to the ghosts.

The basement belongs to another class — a *ghost* class. They don't want to share. And they will haunt Cassidy and her friends until they get their room back!

#1
Ghost Class

Cassidy stumbled over to the wall and flipped on the light switch. She spun around to see a boy about her age, sitting in her desk. He had dark hair that stuck up on top. He wore denim overalls and a striped shirt with a collar. She stared at his tattered shoes until his laughter made her look into his brown eyes.

"How did you do that?" Cassidy asked the boy, but he wouldn't stop laughing. "That wasn't funny at all," she told him.

She stepped toward the desk. "You'd better quit laughing," she warned. She reached over to grab him, but her hand closed around nothing except air — very cold air.

Cassidy's mouth dropped open as she hugged her own dusty arms. She had never felt such a chill. For the first time, Cassidy noticed that the boy wasn't normal. He shimmered around the edges. He was so pale that Cassidy could see right through him. He reminded her of a glowing green-frosted bubble. The boy stood up from the desk and in that instant, he disappeared.

"Where did you go?" Cassidy asked. "Come back here."

The room was still except for a whisper. "I'm warning you. Leave my desk alone."

At first, Cassidy was scared. Had she really seen a ghost? Then Cassidy got mad.

Dust covered every surface of the classroom. Mr. Morton would think she did it. "Come back here and clean up this mess!" Cassidy stomped her foot, sending a little dust cloud into the air above her sneakers. She may as well have been talking to the wind, because the boy didn't reappear.

"This is just great," Cassidy snapped. "Some kids get pen pals — I get a ghost bully."

Suddenly, a noise made Cassidy freeze. Maybe the ghost was back! She whirled around. Jeff and Nina stood at the door to the playground.

"Did you guys see that?" Cassidy asked.

"See what?" Jeff and Nina said together.

"The ghost boy," Cassidy told them.

Jeff laughed. "Yeah, right. I think I just saw a ghost boy skateboarding around the playground."

Nina put her hand on Jeff's shoulder. "I think she's serious. Cassidy really saw something."

"I'm serious, too," Jeff said with a grin. "Serious about the trouble Cassidy's going to be in when Mr. Morton sees this mess. Maybe the Ghostville ghost can help you blast this mess away," he teased.

Cassidy glared at Jeff as she stomped to the back of the room to grab a mop. "I'm not joking," she said. "I just saw a ghost right here in this very classroom."

Jeff tossed a dust mop to Cassidy. "Next you'll think that mop is a dancing skeleton."

"It's not fair," Cassidy mumbled as she swished the mop across the floor. "Not fair. Not fair. Some ghost made the mess and I have to clean it up. Not fair. Not fair. Not fair."

Cassidy stomped on the mat by the back door extra hard. She was so mad she didn't notice that something weird was happening — the little rug underneath her feet was bunching up all on its own. It wiggled, it squirmed, it bubbled, it scrunched. Suddenly, Cassidy teetered. Then she fell down right on the seat of her pants.

From somewhere in the empty basement came the sound of laughter. . . .

Creepy, weird, wacky, and funny things happen to the Bailey School Kids!™ Collect and read them all!

The Adventures of THE BAILEY SCHOOL KIDS®

SCHOLASTIC and associated logos are trademarks and/or registered trademarks of Scholastic Inc.

The Adventures of THE BAILEY SCHOOL KIDS®

❏ BSK 0-439-04398-0   **#38**   **Ninjas Don't Bake Pumpkin Pie** .... $3.99 US
❏ BSK 0-439-04399-9   **#39**   **Dracula Doesn't Rock and Roll** .... $3.99 US
❏ BSK 0-439-04401-4   **#40**   **Sea Monsters Don't Ride Motorcycles** .... $3.99 US
❏ BSK 0-439-04400-6   **#41**   **The Bride of Frankenstein Doesn't**
                        Bake Cookies .... $3.99 US
❏ BSK 0-439-21582-X   **#42**   **Robots Don't Catch Chicken Pox** .... $3.99 US
❏ BSK 0-439-21583-8   **#43**   **Vikings Don't Wear Wrestling Belts** .... $3.99 US
❏ BSK 0-439-21584-6   **#44**   **Ghosts Don't Rope Wild Horses** .... $3.99 US
❏ BSK 0-439-36803-0   **#45**   **Wizards Don't Wear Graduation Gowns** .... $3.99 US
❏ BSK 0-439-36805-7   **#46**   **Sea Serpents Don't Juggle Water Balloons** .... $3.99 US

❏ BSK 0-439-04396-4   **Bailey School Kids Super Special #4:**
                        Mrs. Jeepers in Outer Space .... $3.99 US
❏ BSK 0-439-21585-4   **Bailey School Kids Super Special #5:**
                        Mrs. Jeepers' Monster Class Trip .... $3.99 US
❏ BSK 0-439-30641-8   **Bailey School Kids Super Special #6:**
                        Mrs. Jeepers On Vampire Island .... $3.99 US
❏ BSK 0-439-40831-8   **Bailey School Kids Holiday Special:**
                        Aliens Don't Carve Jack-o'-lanterns .... $3.99 US
❏ BSK 0-439-40832-6   **Bailey School Kids Holiday Special:**
                        Mrs. Claus Doesn't Climb Telephone Poles .... $3.99 US
❏ BSK 0-439-33338-5   **Bailey School Kids Thanksgiving Special:**
                        Swamp Monsters Don't Chase Wild Turkeys .... $3.99 US

Available wherever you buy books, or use this order form

Scholastic Inc., P.O. Box 7502, Jefferson City, MO 65102

Please send me the books I have checked above. I am enclosing $_____ (please add $2.00 to cover shipping and handling). Send check or money order — no cash or C.O.D.s please.

Name _____

Address _____

City _____ State/Zip _____

Please allow four to six weeks for delivery. Offer good in the U.S. only. Sorry, mail orders are not available to residents of Canada. Prices subject to change.

BSK902

MORE SERIES YOU'LL FALL IN LOVE WITH

GET READY FOR GABI!

Gabi is a lucky girl. She can speak English *and* Spanish. But some days, when things get crazy, Gabi's words get all mixed-up!

In a family of superstars, it's hard to stand out. But Abby is about to surprise her friends, her family, and most of all, herself!

The AMAZING DAYS of ABBY HAYES®

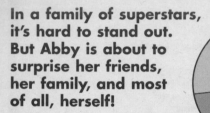

Ghostville Elementary™

Welcome to Sleepy Hollow Elementary! Everyone says the basement is haunted, but no one's ever gone downstairs to prove it. Until now...

This year, Jeff and Cassidy's classroom is moving to the basement—the creepy, haunted basement. And you thought your school was scary...?

Learn more at **www.scholastic.com/books**

Available Wherever Books Are Sold.

SCHOLASTIC

LAPT1